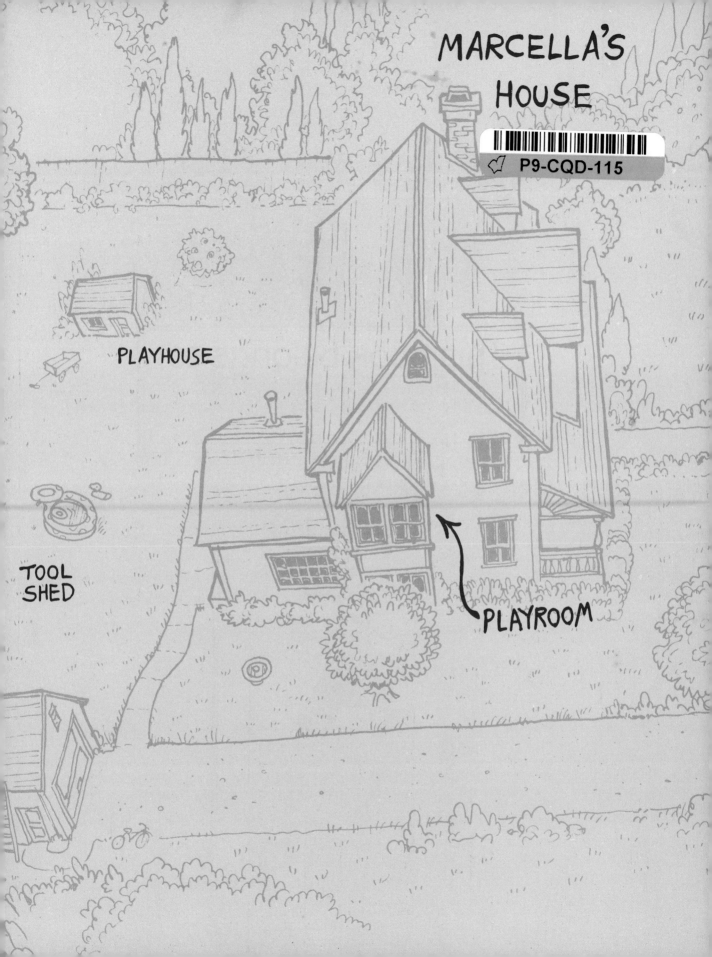

MARCELLA'S HOUSE

P9-CQD-115

PLAYHOUSE

TOOL SHED

PLAYROOM

This book belongs to:

_____

Raggedy Ann & Andy's

BUBBLES GOES TO THE FAIR

A LYNX BOOK

Copyright © 1988 Macmillan, Inc. All rights reserved. No part of this book may be reproduced or transmitted in any form or by any means without the written permission of the Publisher. Printed in the United States of America.   ISBN: 1-55802-118-3   0 9 8 7 6 5 4 3 2

This book is published by Lynx Books, a division of Lynx Communications, Inc., 41 Madison Avenue, New York, New York 10010. The name "Lynx" together with the logotype consisting of a stylized head of a lynx is a trademark of Lynx Communications, Inc.

Raggedy Ann and Andy's Grow-and-Learn Library, the names and depictions of Raggedy Ann, Raggedy Andy and all related characters are trademarks of Macmillan, Inc.

Shh. Bubbles the Clown Doll got up and tiptoed across the room. It was early morning, and the other playroom dolls were still fast asleep. Bubbles didn't make a sound as he picked up his juggling balls . . .

and tossed them into the air. Bubbles was getting ready for his big moment. Today he was going to the Raggedy Land Fair. He was going to enter the juggling contest, which he very much wanted to win.

Bubbles practiced in the silent playroom. The balls went up in a circle. Red, blue, green, red, blue . . .

Whoops! The green ball bounced out of Bubbles' hand and landed on Raggedy Ann's bed. Uh-oh!

"Sorry!" Bubbles whispered as the little ball tapped Raggedy Ann on her shoulder.

"Good morning, Bubbles," answered Raggedy Ann. "Why are you up so early?" she asked.

"I'm excited about the contest!" he said.

"I'm sure you'll win a prize," Raggedy Ann told him. "You've been practicing every day for weeks!"

As Bubbles and Raggedy Ann talked, the other dolls and toys began to wake up. They rolled out of their beds and hopped off their shelves. They climbed out of the toy box.

"I can't wait to get to the fair!" cried Greta the Dutch Doll.

"I can't wait to enter the jump-rope contest," said Sunny Bunny, who could jump better than anyone else.
Everyone in the playroom was looking forward to the fair.

Raggedy Ann and Raggedy Andy were going to enter the three-legged race together.

Babette the French Doll helped Raggedy Dog get ready for the dog show. She brushed his raggedy patches until he looked brand new.

Raggedy Dog wagged his tail and stared into the big mirror. "Maybe I *will* win a ribbon at the Raggedy Land Fair, after all," he thought.

Raggedy Andy was looking into the dollhouse kitchen and watching Mrs. Small bake her pie.

Suddenly, Percy the Policeman Doll announced that it was nine o'clock! It was time to leave for the Raggedy Land Fair.

Raggedy Andy picked up Mrs. Small and carried her and her little pie. Raggedy Ann picked up her sack for the race. Bubbles the Clown tossed his juggling balls neatly into a little bag—one, two, three!

As the group gathered at the playroom door, Raggedy Ann took a last look around.

"Oops!" she cried. "Sunny Bunny has forgotten his jump rope!"

"Don't worry," said Bubbles, setting down his bag. "I'll get it." And he rushed back to the table.

All the dolls headed merrily down the back stairs and
out the kitchen door.

They crossed the yard and ran through the Deep Deep
Woods. Along the way they saw their friends the sparrows.

They ran all the way to Raggedy Land.

Up ahead they saw the patchwork tents and the balloons and the banners.

"I can't wait to play ringtoss," shouted Raggedy Andy.

"I want to hear the band play music," said Tim the Toy Soldier.

They all wanted to do everything right away, and they hadn't even arrived yet!

Bubbles ran right up to the stage where a magic show had begun. He was about to sit down when he heard a voice over the loudspeaker.

"The juggling contest is about to begin! All contestants should report to the red tent."

That was when Bubbles realized that he'd left his juggling balls behind.

"Oh, no!" he moaned. He remembered that his bag was back on the playroom floor.

"What will I do? Someone has to help me." He felt disappointed and annoyed with himself.

"Sunny Bunny!" he thought. Bubbles knew he had gone back for Sunny Bunny's jump rope. Maybe now Sunny Bunny would go back for his juggling balls. But Sunny Bunny had already started jumping rope. Bubbles couldn't ask him to help now.

"Maybe Babette could help me," Bubbles said to himself, finding his way to the dog show. But Babette was busy tying a big bow on Raggedy Dog before he stepped onto the stage. He couldn't ask either of them.

"On your mark, get set, GO!" The three-legged race had begun.

Raggedy Ann and Raggedy Andy were off to a good start.

"Good luck!" yelled Bubbles. He just couldn't ask them to help him now either.

Poor Bubbles! Everyone was busy! And the juggling contest had begun.

"What am I going to do?" he asked himself. "I just have to be in that contest. I guess if no one else can help me, I'll have to help myself!"

He sat down to think.

Bubbles twiddled his thumbs and thought, "There must be a way. . . . There must be a way. . . ."

While Bubbles was twiddling, he was watching Tina the Patchwork Turtle close her eyes and bob for apples in the big tin tub.

PLOP! went Tina.

HOP! went Bubbles as he jumped up from the ground. He had a great idea.

"I've got it!" Bubbles shouted. The rosy round apples would make perfect juggling balls!

"May I borrow three apples, Mr. Blackbird?" Bubbles asked.

"Of course, Bubbles!" Mr. Blackbird answered.

Bubbles scooped up three apples from the ground and ran as fast as he could. He reached the juggling tent just as the contest was about to end. With a quick flip of his wrist . . .

the three apples bounced into the air. Up and down. Round and round. Bubbles juggled the best he ever had!

"We have a winner!" said a booming voice over the loudspeaker. "The winner is—

Bubbles the Clown!"

The audience cheered. His friends cheered.

Bubbles held up his prize. "I won! I won!" He thought to himself, "I won because I helped myself. What a great day!"

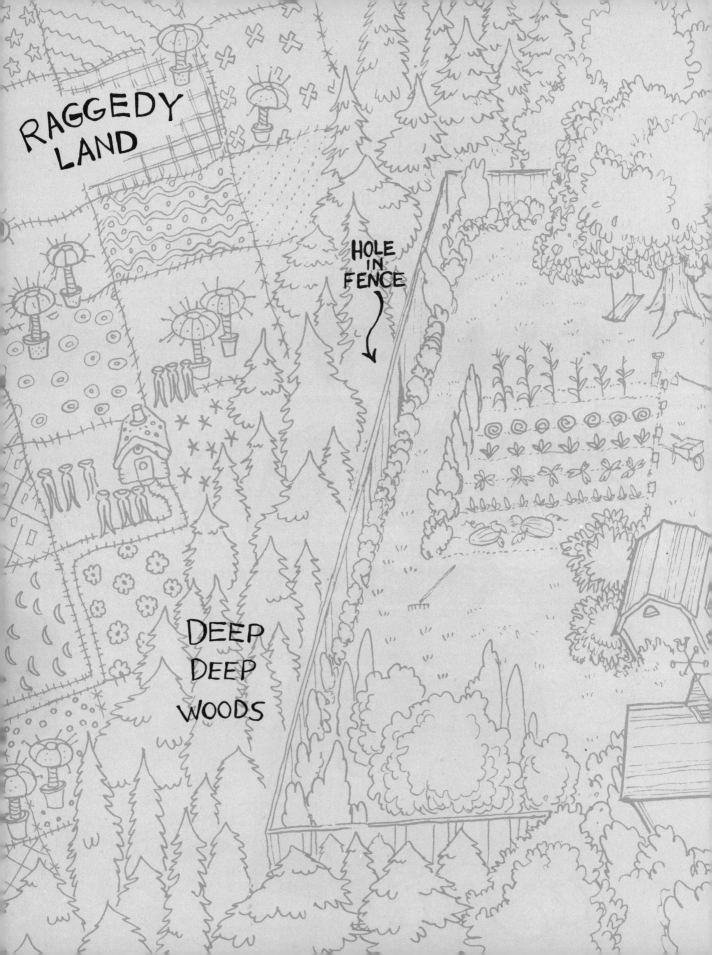

RAGGEDY
LAND

HOLE
IN
FENCE

DEEP
DEEP
WOODS